The Mysterious Musings
of a
Precarious Heart

by

S.J. Dennery
&
Mila A. Ballentine

ISBN: 978-0-9889725-3-7

PUBLISHER'S NOTE

This novel is a work of fiction told from the perspective of fictitious
character experiences. The names, places and characters are products
of the author's imagination. Any resemblance to actual persons living
or dead, business establishments, event or locals is coincidental.

DEDICATION

I dedicate this book to my mother.

PROLOGUE

"Secrets are never buried until the keeper of those secrets is dead."- S.J. Dennery

ONE

Hues of the aurora faded and the moon took over the sky casting a shadow on a rooftop with red shingles. She lay back against the grainy surface. Her dreadlock extensions flared casting a faint shadow behind her. Worry lines made themselves at home on her face and her thoughts lingered into places where she felt haunted by someone else's circumstance.

"Lilac." Her mother's raspy voice traveled outside.

She edged down the roof, parted her sheer blue curtains, and climbed inside her bedroom window. "Yes, Mom."

The petite woman with light freckles dotting her olive cheeks managed a guarded smile. "I was just checking on you."

"I'm fine." Lilac's foot dragged along the green carpet before she crawled back out to the roof. She sat there and took in the moon for a while but yawns soon intervened. Her head lowered and her eyelids drifted to a close. Lilac's head jerked backwards as her reflexes kicked in and she opened her eyes. A low groan followed as she crawled back inside the house. She leapt into her bed, pulled the sheets up to her neck, and slowly drifted into a deep sleep.

The synchronized rhythm of the wind motioned the limb of a nearby tree to claw at the glass in the window frame. The dull light of the morning sun lay on her face highlighting her freckles. Her hair flared like porcupine quills from beneath. The sheet slipped from her as she turned; Lilac got out of bed, and went downstairs to prowl for breakfast before entering the wild jungles of Vanderlin High School.

She opened the fridge, took out a can of sardines, opened it, and tilted it to her mouth. The slick sardines slipped over the rim into her lips and slid down her esophagus into the valley of degradable food. Lilac tossed the empty sardine can in the garbage and went back upstairs to get ready. She looked in the dresser mirror and sported a grin that displayed teeth encased in a sequence of sparkling braces.

Miniature dolls clung to the peach walls in her bedroom amongst pictures of the rudimentary drawings of people who she had sketched over the years. There was one doll in particular that she'd started to sew years ago, but was unable to finish it. Lilac picked up that doll from her dresser. She'd named it after someone she'd gotten to know over the years; someone who had become a dear friend. Lilac went through her things and placed an outfit on the bed. She got dressed and looked at herself in the mirror, admiring the black t-shirt, zebra pants and black combat boots she put together. She saw a reflection behind her in the mirror and jumped. "You scared me."

"It's 6:45! Hurry up before you're late for school."
Ruby's voice traveled across the hall.

"I'm coming." Lilac grabbed her bag.

She scampered down the staircase and left the house,
letting the screen door slam behind her in her haste. She
hopped on her mint green 50cc scooter with silver stripes
on each side. The smell of burnt rubber wafted through
the air as the rear tire spun with the front wheel locked.
An ear rattling noise resonated behind her as she sped off
down Zephyr Street.

Lilac coasted toward Vanderlin High School, a three-
story building with towering turrets and gargoyles that
guarded the unruly students from the roof's edge. Its
stony façade reminded her of the castles in Europe but the
students who walked the halls were far from regal. They
could be downright animalistic at times. Lilac drove
through the lot and parked her scooter. She took off her
helmet as she walked to the entrance and sifted through
the crowd of students.

His spiky black hair stuck out from beneath the front of
his red hoodie. He walked down the dimly lit hallway.
Her nemesis, Lester's, opaque skin made her skin crawl.
He was the *emo* prince from hell. She glared at him from
the corner of her eye. A thick line of black eyeliner
outlined his gray eyes and a silver lip ring stuck out of the
left side of his lips. As he walked past her, her head sunk
into her shoulders and her heart raced. She exhaled when
he passed by without acknowledging her presence.

TWO

Her first and second period classes went by, and before she knew it, she was strolling into her third period class. Lilac joined the other students loafing around the room. Mr. Coors walked through a side entrance and stood in front of the class. He was dressed in a light blue polo shirt and a pair of dark blue polyester shorts that highlighted the bright blond hairs that curled like waves against his muscular legs. He lifted the whistle that dangled from his neck and blew.

Pacing in front of the students he said, "We have a test coming up on Friday on the fundamentals of lacrosse. I made arrangements for you to play on the lacrosse team." Mr. Coors stopped pacing and stood in the path of a beam of light that came through a skylight in the roof. The sun's rays landed on his head blotting out his short blond hair and a portion of his face. Chuckles rippled through the gymnasium. Mr. Coors was staring right at them but all they saw was the glare.

"What are you waiting for? Go on and get dressed!" Mr. Coors walked to the bleachers and sat down.

The students dispersed and went into their locker rooms. As soon as Lilac walked inside, the girls grabbed their belongings and left. They wanted nothing to do with a Genmorph, a genetically engineered breed, especially at school. Lilac's DNA was spliced with chameleon and troll DNA, but she didn't care about the specifics of her existence. She was content as long as she could breathe. Lilac put on her gym clothes and walked out to the field where the rest of her classmates lined up to select their equipment. They were being paired up with players from the lacrosse team.

She spotted a critter near the bleachers and charged toward it. Lilac grabbed the beetle by the leg. With the flick of her nails she set it on fire and blew out the flame. She sprinkled salt and pepper on the beetle from small packets that she happened to have in her pocket. Lilac put the bug in her mouth and munched. The beetle's gooey caramelized flavor gushed in her mouth. She couldn't help herself; the troll side of her had uncontrollable urges to eat bugs like candy.

A young man who sat at the end of the bleachers looked at her with wide eyes. Nardo couldn't believe that a girl as beautiful as her could eat a bug without hesitation. Lilac looked over her shoulder and saw him walking in her direction. His complexion was like a block of caramel candy and his hazel-brown eyes screamed sexy. Nardo's short curly brown hair made her want to run her fingers through his mane. His body looked like it was carved out of mahogany and the muscles on his legs flexed handsomely as he walked.

"Are you Lilac?"

"Yup, that's me?"

"I'm Nardo. I'll be your partner for the week."

Thank God, I got a cute one. "Great."

From the moment they slipped on their gear and positioned themselves on the field, it was no holds barred. The ball was pelted down the glistening green field in her direction and she stepped aside letting it float right past her. While observing the students, Mr. Coors saw her ignore the ball. He blew his whistle. There was no way she was going to let a gang of boys that were thirsty for a win toss her around. They were having too much fun at the girls' expense. The girls rolled their eyes and picked at their nails. "Come on Paine, chase the ball!" Lilac could see the uvula between of his tonsils as he shouted.

Lilac's faced reddened. She ran down the field, cupped the ball in the basket and threw it to Nardo. After a half hour of chasing boys and balls, Mr. Coors finally blew the whistle. It was music to her ears. She put away her equipment and rushed to the locker room. Lilac couldn't wait to take a shower.

After a workout in gym she often looked like a wet noodle. Lilac felt icky drenched in her sweat. She entered the locker room. Steam clogged the walkway that led to the showers, and the sweet aroma of peaches lingered around a redheaded teenage girl named Janelle, that was covered in suds. Water beat against her pear-shaped gazelle frame and cascaded down to her feet.

Lilac peeled off her clothes, got in the shower and an unpleasant odor fumed. Water slid off Lilac's hair, as if it was afraid to venture through her thick, lint infested dreadlock extensions. The only thing that distinguished their showers from those in prison was the complimentary fabric shower curtains that came with a hint of mildew.

Janelle sniffed the air. She couldn't escape the stench fuming from the shower next to her but she had a plan. She gave Lilac a handful of miniature soaps that she collected from hotels that her family visited while they were on vacation. "Thanks, Janelle."

"It's my pleasure."

They weren't close, but Lilac was the first person she had encountered on her first day in Vanderlin High School. Lilac took the time to escort her to her first period class. Janelle saw firsthand that Lilac was a gentle soul, even though she didn't show it half the time. She wanted Lilac to get compliments about how good she smelled. If her stench was allowed to fester, everyone would have to pay the price.

Laughter from the boy's locker room trickled into theirs, but their laughs soon morphed into something else.

"Snake— Snake!" They shouted and pranced as the bronze snake slid across the floor.

Lilac gasped, *Sugar.* She let her out before she entered the gymnasium. Lilac ran to the boy's locker room, "Don't touch my snake!" She parted her way through a crowd of bare chested teenage boys wrapped in pristine white towels that draped just below their navels.

"This?" Nardo held it.

"Can I have my snake, please?" She glared at him.

"You sure can. If I didn't catch it, your pet would've bitten someone."

She took Sugar from his grasp and he got a whiff of her. It was an upgrade from the death-defying funk she was sporting earlier. Nardo stared at her torso.

Shit! She was so hell bent on retrieving Sugar that she didn't realize she only had a towel on. Lilac rolled her eyes and walked away with her snake. She worked up an appetite during Gym class. Thankfully, her lunch hour was next. Lilac walked past a line of tables, sat down and took a bite of her rice wrap.

It reminded her of the class trip her Foreign Language class took last year to Korea. It was a fond memory. If she could, she would like to live there. The Genmorph population was larger there and they morphed out in public without any repercussions. She had the pleasure of morphing while she was there. Her eyes bulged, allowing her to tap into her 360-degree arc vision. Her olive skin faded and a glossy coat of blue-orange and turquoise-green with a sliver of brown stripes surfaced. It was a beautiful sight to see. She could never do that back home. It was harder to fit in at school, let alone, a small town like Charleston, Oregon where the number of Genmorphs had rapidly decreased over the years. She ate the rest of her food and left the Cafeteria.

* * *

Nardo wasn't exactly ecstatic about going to his next class. It was one of the hardest classes for him to get through. He entered and sat in the middle of the classroom. Mrs. Peen rambled away as Nardo nodded into a light sleep. Her World History discussions always bordered on the epiphany of boredom and the students suffered for it. Today, she decided to bore them with environmental details.

"Much of what happened was redacted from the public records, but if you ask an elder in any community you'd find that our environment suffered greatly from ground and air pollutants. In mankind's desperate attempt to save our atmosphere, the superpowers enacted a top secret plan called Massive Air Purification Systems, M.A.P.S, that cost billions of dollars to decontaminate the air we breathe. The level of carbon dioxide in the atmosphere had risen by fifteen percent and it didn't include what we contribute. Colossal purifiers were constructed in military installations throughout the world. M.A.P.S worked beyond their expectations but it decreased oxygen and increased carbon dioxide to dangerous levels in the atmosphere within the matter of a decade. Those who were once relatively healthy became ill; they experienced dizziness, nausea, blindness or worse, death."

"Can anyone tell me why that is a problem?"

Liberty raised her hand. Coke bottle glasses drowned her slender face, but her short brunette pixie haircut made her stand out in a room. Mrs. Peen pointed to her.

"Carbon dioxide is toxic when it's above the normal level in the atmosphere. The same is true for oxygen."

"That's correct. Thank you, Liberty."

"Many died, but some did whatever they had to do to survive. To make matters worse, natural selection was not left to run its course. Scientist found a way for humans to adapt to the new environment. Some citizens offered their bodies for research and the changes they endured were unlike any other subjects that had come before them.

The number of people who opted out of the process was far greater than those who participated. They were later coined the Normals; humans who were unchanged by mankind's meddling with genetics. Afterwards, they wished things could go back to the way it had been, but it was too late. They were stuck in the fresh world that they created."

The bell rang; Nardo eased out of his seat, tossed his backpack over his shoulder and left the room. He left school and rode to his after school job. On the south side of the building, Lilac filtered through a sea of students as she exited the building. She walked to the parking lot, hopped on her scooter and left school. Her green scooter puttered to a stop halfway home and wouldn't start again.

Lilac pushed the scooter to the nearest auto repair shop, which was only fifteen minutes away by foot. She parked her scooter outside Clyde's Auto Shop. She glanced at the white paint that flaked off of the wood siding, a pan of motor oil lay on the floor near a black *Volkswagen* Jetta with its hood open, and grease smudged various spots on the inner walls. The owner, a bald stocky older man in blue overalls and a white vest shuffled out of a room in the back. "What do you need?"

"My scooter broke down."

"Hold on. I'll get my grandson to look at it."

"Bernardo!" He yelled and wiped sweat from his brow with a handkerchief. "We have a customer with scooter issues."

He looked at Lilac. "Bring your scooter inside." He walked back inside, but Lilac didn't budge. He turned to her. "What are you waiting for? You expect an old man like me to do it?"

She rolled her eyes while following him with the scooter.

Nardo slid from underneath a car he was working on and got up.

"What brings you here?"

"My scooter quit on me. Can you fix it?"

"I'll take a look. You can have a seat outside." Nardo escorted her to a line of seats near the entrance next to an old coffee table with a selection of old magazines.

"I'd rather watch."

"I'm sorry, but that's not allowed."

"How long is this going to take?"

"Give or take about fifteen to twenty minutes."

Lilac sat down and watched cars driving by. She picked up a Collectable Automobile magazine, flipped through it and put it aside. She hadn't been there long, but time seemed to be crawling by. Lilac looked at her watch and reached for another magazine. Sugar slithered out of her school bag, moved toward Nardo, circled him, and coiled around his leg. "Get this thing off of me!"

Lilac released Sugar from his leg.

"She's harmless. Are you done?" Lilac asked.

"Just about." He fastened a bolt and put his tools away. "Now you're good to go."

"Great! What's the damage?"

Nardo wiped the grease off of his hands with an old rag and looked at her. "It's on me."

"Really?" She wasn't looking for a freebie.

Nardo nodded.

"Thank you for fixing my scooter, bye." Lilac got on the scooter, revved the engine and waved as she drove away.

Nardo stood in his workspace, watching her get smaller as she drove away. She was so distant toward him, but he understood why. If she knew what he'd done, she would be nicer to him. He'd witnessed one jerk in particular, Lester, making fun of Lilac, from her hair down to her boots in between classes. Nardo waited until he and Lester were alone in lacrosse and he elbowed him in the gut. They tumbled to the ground and Nardo pressed his lacrosse stick to Lester's throat. "If you ever bother her again, I'll bench press your face."

After that incident, Lester didn't bother her but Nardo almost got himself kicked off the team. Lester wasn't the only person who taunted her, but he was the most extravagant. It got so bad that Nardo noticed Lilac's defense mechanisms unfolding and she'd almost shown her true form in school. As far as anyone knew, she looked like every other human being, but he saw her for who she really was.

It was the beginning of the many strange things that continued to unfold in *Charleston, Oregon*. In the last six months, the environment at school had steadily gone downhill. Everyone knew why but no one dared to say. Nardo realized how dangerous that could be when he witnessed a modern day witch-hunt of a Genmorph who'd revealed his true self at school. His name was Richard, and Nardo hadn't seen him since the incident.

* * *

Lilac puttered down Zephyr Street on her green scooter and parked in the garage. She entered the house and tossed her keys in a basket on the kitchen counter.

"You're late. Where were you?"

"The scooter broke down and I had to get it fixed." Lilac removed her bag from her shoulder and rested it on the rug.

"What's wrong?"

"Nothing. I'm just tired."

After eating a light supper with her mom, Lilac ran up the stairs and crash-landed on her bed. She lay on her tummy watching the green minerals float around inside the lava lamp on the table. Her eyelids fluttered for a while before closing. The chime of car alarms in the distance woke her as debris from a meteor shower pelted to the ground.

Lilac crawled out of bed and walked over to the window. She stood there admiring the moon. Falling stars skipped across the skyline before plummeting to earth. It was a beautiful site but she needed rest if she had any intentions of surviving school tomorrow. She changed into her pajamas and went back to bed. Her fleece Betty Boop pajamas tugged at the cotton sheets as she climbed in bed and closed her eyes leaving a night of atmospheric splendor behind.

The sturdy roar of the alarm clock had been rattling for the past twenty minutes before she pressed the snooze button, except the clock was at the other end of the room. She was asleep but Lilac envisioned her hand stretching through thin air, pressing the button and having the noise stop. Ruby stood at Lilac's open door dressed in a peach lace-trimmed nightgown and had green curlers in her hair that were covered by a crocheted hair net. She sighed as she looked at Lilac, encased in a cocoon made of dried skin, with threads of silk spun around the outer layer.

Lilac's cocoon moved slowly beneath the sheets. Ruby entered the room. "Rise and shine." The alarm clock continued whining. "Get up and turn the clock off." Ruby shook her. She didn't budge.

"Are you okay?"

The cocoon cracked and Lilac broke out of her shell.

Ruby touched Lilac; she was as cold as ice.

Lilac's eyes opened, "Hi, Mom. I'm fine."

"That's good to hear. Now get up and get ready for school."

Lilac sat up, wobbled over to the clock and turned it off. She went into the bathroom and washed her face.

18

Ruby peeked inside the bathroom. Ever since puberty took its course, Lilac had gone through phases that involved shedding her skin and occasional rebirths where she'd end up in cocoons, but Ruby never got used to it.

"You look exhausted. Go back to bed. I'll take you to school later."

"Thanks Mom." Lilac kissed her mother on the cheek, and went back to bed.

She woke hours later, strolled into the bathroom and looked at her reflection in the mirror. The sight of her reflection brought her to tears. *You're an ugly troll, Lilac Paine*. Lester's words still echoed in her head. It was one of the many unfortunate experiences she had gone through during her adolescence.

There was a time when she didn't want to go to school but it wasn't an option. Lester seemed to devote his life to making her life miserable, and each time he'd go the extra mile. He made fun of her hair, called her *the creature from the black lagoon* and turned a trash can over on her head. She came home that day in tears and collapsed in her mother's arms. In those moments, Ruby felt utterly helpless, and Lilac saw something in her mother's eyes that she'd never seen before.

That was the last straw; Ruby vowed to go down to the middle school and handle it herself but Lilac begged her not to go berserk at her school. The hardest thing for a parent to endure, outside of the loss of a child, is not being able to help them. Ruby scheduled a meeting with the principal. She was stoic after their talk. Ruby spent the rest of the day lamenting.

"I don't get it. He basically said that punishment was reserved for the end of the school year. They would take away end-of-the-year function privileges. That's a load of crap! It encourages bullies to terrorize their victims without consequences in the meantime."

Things settled down for a week, but Lester went back to his old tactics. Weeks later he stopped bothering her. She didn't know why, but she didn't care as long as he left her alone.

Lilac grabbed a pair of scissors and chopped her dreadlock extensions off, one by one. After twelve minutes of cutting her hair, she began to recognize the girl she knew three years ago. Lilac dried her eyes and got dressed. She traipsed downstairs in a green Hell Bunny mini skirt that bounced over white- and green-striped tights, and walked to the garage.

Ruby started the tan Volvo and drove her to school. Lilac could feel the heat from the brown leather seat through her stockings. Ruby didn't talk on the ride over so Lilac spent the time finger drumming on the side door. The car pulled into the driveway in front of Vanderlin High School's main office and Lilac got out.

"Don't forget to call the attendance office. See you later, Mom." Lilac closed the car door, walked to the double glass doors and entered the building.

She went to her unit office, got a pass and walked to her fourth period classroom. The bell rang as she stepped up to Mrs. Smith's room. She waited until the students came out before entering to get her homework and then she went to the rest of the classes that she missed earlier.

THREE

Nardo's first period class dragged on, but eventually it was over and he couldn't wait for his next class to end. He rushed out at the sound of the bell and hustled to the gymnasium. He entered the gym and walked into the locker room. His teammates were swatting one another with towels but Nardo wasn't in the mood for horseplay. He got dressed and walked out to the field. Nardo visually scanned the area. *Where is she?*

Renaldo tapped him on the shoulder. "Let's go. Practice starts in five minutes."

"I'm coming."

Renaldo's stocky frame bolted across the field and joined the other players. Nardo soon took off behind him. Playing the game with their own lacrosse members was a breeze compared to playing in Mr. Coors class. *It's too bad*. After today, they'd go back to playing amongst themselves.

* * *

The mood in the cafeteria seemed more festive than usual. A succession of claps and whistles erupted around the tables where the cheer team congregated with the lacrosse team. "Yeah Team." Their pom pom's twisted in the air.

The air in the cafeteria was colder than usual and it didn't take long for the chill to spread like a yawn in a room. The lights flickered and went out. The room filled with fervent chatter.

"Turn the lights back on."

The lights came on, but the chill remained. Lilac sat down and took out an avocado sandwich. Nardo saw her and walked over to her.

"Can we talk?" He sat in front of her.

"I'm busy."

Nardo got up.

"You have five minutes. Let's talk outside." She finished her sandwich and got up. They walked through the double doors and went through a side door into the courtyard.

"I like your new hairstyle. It looks good on you."

"I bet you tell that to all the girls at school."

"I'd be lying if I said you were the first, but I meant what I said. Is everything okay with you? You didn't show up for practice."

"I'm good."

"Can I have your phone number?"

"No."

"Come on, Lilac, go easy on me."

"599-1313."

Nardo entered her number into his contacts.

"What's yours?" Lilac pulled out a notebook.

"695-2246. You can call me whenever you like."

She smiled, "You're the first guy's number that I've gotten without a group project being the culprit."

"Really?"

"Yeah."

"Things are different now."

The fifth bell rang. "I have to go to class.

"Can I give you a ride home later?" Nardo twirled his keys on his index finger.

"Sure."

He walked with her to the building. They paused once they got inside the door. "My class is down the hall." Lilac adjusted her textbook in her hand.

"My class is at the other end of the hall. We should meet here after school. It will save me the trouble of having to look for you."

"I'll see you later." Lilac went into her classroom and Nardo walked down the hall.

The class was separated into four groups. Lilac's face lit up when she saw that they'd be dissecting frogs. The other girls in the class scrunched up their faces. Trixie sat across from her on their table. She was as close to a mythical beast that she'd ever seen with her rainbow colored hair and she had a habit of emitting gas in class. She dropped farts like napalm and then she'd walk away like nothing ever happened. The odor was so putrid that Lilac could tell exactly what she'd eaten; *steak and eggs with a hint of butt*. Her nose scrunched as the aroma misted up her nasal passage.

Trixie twitched in her chair. Lilac looked at her sideways. What was left of Trixie's steak and eggs came gushing out of her mouth and it mixed with the nauseating odor of the preservative used to soak the specimens. The teacher walked over and placed a roll of paper towels on their table. Trixie held her nose, stooped down and cleaned up her bile.

Lilac focused on the frog sprawled out on the tray. She put her hand up and volunteered to dissect it. The rest of the group squinted their eyes as Lilac made a gash down the center of the frog. It had all of the essential parts, a heart and lung amongst other things. They had so much in common but were still vastly different. She exhaled; thankfully she was on the better end of the deal with the knife and not below. Dissecting a frog was less interesting once she wrapped her mind around that concept.

She was relieved when the bell rang and her classmates shared her enthusiasm. Her last class was the least of her worries unless there was someone who didn't want to do their part. All she had to do was help the other students with their cooking assignments. Those were the moments where she wished she had the ability to grade a student. She'd give the slackers an *F* for failing to follow through with an assignment.

Everyone appeared to be doing their part. Today's assignment involved making spaghetti. Lilac walked by Ashley's table and looked inside the pot. "Where's the water?"

"I don't know."

"Did you add water?"

"Yes I did."

Lilac stood there looking at her and shook her head. Ashley had put a pot of water on the burner and stared at it until it dried out.

"Why didn't you ask for help?"

"I was daydreaming and before I knew it the water was gone." Soap Opera tears dripped off of her eyelids.

The rest of the students chuckled. Lilac glared at her. "Clean up your station."

The bell rang as Lilac walked away from Ashley's table. Ashley picked up her bag, walked out of the classroom and left the pot smoking on the burner. Lilac hustled over, turned off the burner and removed the pot.

Mrs. Miles sighed. "I don't know what to do with that girl. She doesn't seem to care about anything."

Lilac silently got her bag and left the class. She walked down the hall and opened the metal door. Nardo stood off to the side on the lawn. Lilac went over to him and they walked to his motorbike.

She sat behind him and held on to his waist. He revved the engine and drove out of the lot. A few minutes into the ride, Nardo heard strange sounds behind his ear.

"What are you doing?"

"I'm eating bugs."

"Where did you get bugs?"

"I opened my mouth and waited for the critters to arrive."

"Okay, I get the idea."

She giggled and tightened her grip on his waist. Nardo stopped at the traffic light, his feet left the pedal and rested on the asphalt but Lilac continued to hold on to his waist like she was about to slip off the edge.

"Loosen your hold on me before my lunch backs up."

"Sorry." Lilac giggled.

The light turned green and they zipped down the street before turning on Zephyr Street. A short time later, he parked outside her house. He glanced at her two story cream house with the red roof. Crape myrtle trees stood at both sides of the house proudly showing their purple flowers, and lavender lined the areas between the steps along the front porch.

Lilac got off and stepped up on the sidewalk. "Thanks for the ride."

"You're welcome." He adjusted his helmet and drove away from her residence.

Lilac waved as he drove away. Ruby sat on the porch in a light robe taking in the cool afternoon air.

"Who's he?"

"A friend."

"If you say so."

"Really Mom; he's just a friend."

Lilac went inside, sat down on the sleigh couch with an Aztec print and stared at the wood shelf pressed against the wall. It was starting to look like the trinket fortress. A pig on skates, a glass monkey, two giraffes with legs that dangled from pins and a ceramic joker adorned in silk garments were the latest addition to Ruby's ornament sanctuary. Lilac shook her head and opened her textbook.

Ruby entered the living room. "It wouldn't be the end of the world if you liked him."

"I know Mom, but I have work to do."

"And besides —"

"Mom, we're just friends. Why would he be interested in dating a Genmorph when he could have any girl?"

"I won't mention it again."

Lilac grabbed her books, jogged up the stairs, and closed her door.

* * *

Two miles away, Nardo stood beneath the showerhead as suds slid down his body and into the drain. He turned off the water, stepped out and put on his favorite pajama pants that hung low on his waist. The aroma of butter sizzling with julienned garlic, followed by a hint of the sea traveled upstairs. Nardo took in the aroma and hurried downstairs.

His mom placed plates of Shrimp Scampi on the table, Nardo sat down and they ate dinner together.

His dad glanced at him. "How's school going?"

"Okay."

"I'm glad to hear that. The last thing you need is to get into trouble."

"May I be excused?"

"Sure."

Nardo got up from the table, carried his empty plate to the kitchen and put it in the sink. He went upstairs to his room and lay back on his bed, removed his phone from his pocket and sorted through his contacts. He stopped at her name and selected talk. After a succession of rings, someone picked up on the other end. Nardo gently said, "Lilac?"

"You have reached the Rejection Hotline. The person who gave you this number would rather kiss a frog than talk to you. You're wasting your time. There are other tadpoles in the pond; find one who actually likes you. Goodbye."

Nardo hung up. "That crank gave me the wrong number." He tossed his phone at the side of the bed and stared at the ceiling. It soon faded to black as he drifted into a deep sleep.

* * *

His eyes opened to the sound of the alarm clock the next day. Nardo hesitated before he got up. He walked up to one of his posters that was falling off the wall and pressed the tape tight to the wall. Nardo went to the bathroom to brush his teeth. He combed his hair and went downstairs. His mother stood in front of the sink drying dishes and placing them in the cabinet. He kissed her on the cheek. Her smooth porcelain skin felt cold as his lips touched her.

"Good Morning."

"Morning sweetie. Did you get a good night's rest?" Her blonde ponytail wagged as she turned to him.

"Not exactly, but I slept."

"Is there something you'd like to talk about?"

"Not really." Nardo grabbed an apple out of the fruit bowl on the counter and bit into it.

"I'll see you later."

He left the house, got on his blue Kawasaki motorbike and drove to school. Nardo whisked through the chilly morning air for the half-hour drive to school. He was used to the weather, but the older generation missed the feel of summer. He didn't know any better; their generation only experienced fall and spring. He'd often heard his grandfather talk about the way things were back when he was a boy.

Ice storms had crippled cities and closed airports, but he'd never seen a lick of snow. He pulled into the parking lot outside the cafeteria and parked his motorbike. When Nardo entered, the hot air in the hall hugged his face. He entered the cafeteria and stood in line.

Lilac entered just in time before breakfast was over. She walked through a row of tables to the lineup area, grabbed a pop tart and a banana and purchased it at the checkout. Nardo got up from his seat to get ketchup for his hash browns. Lilac saw Nardo and walked to him.

"Hi, Nardo."

He didn't respond.

"Nardo?"

He dropped the ketchup in the container and walked back to his table. Nardo stopped at the end of a line of tables and sat down.

I've done it this time. He was the only guy at school who was nice to me and I've totally blew it. Maybe it was for the best.

Nardo tried to push her out of his thoughts as he went on with his day. He daydreamed his way through most of his classes but all he could think about was her eager brown eyes and dark hair that curved just behind her ear. He sighed and tapped his forehead on the desk a few times. His life would be easier if he could get that nutty girl out of his head. The bell rang and he got out of there. Nardo drove home and relaxed for a while.

* * *

He put on a jump suit and took his dog, Sweeper, out for a walk. It soon turned into a run when Sweeper spotted a squirrel. His ears flapped in the wind as he ran. The feisty bugger ran up a tree and Sweeper's barks echoed through the neighborhood. Sweat from Nardo's upper body soaked the rim of his pants. Sweeper tugged him along by his leash down the sidewalk. They turned the corner and walked down Zephyr Street. He stopped in front of Lilac's house. Nardo stooped down and looked into Sweeper's eyes.

"Do you think I should go see her?" His dog rolled over and growled.

"Good boy, Sweeper. I guess I could talk to her."

Inside, Lilac applied hair removal cream and scraped it off with a plastic putty knife.

"Lilac, you have a visitor." Ruby called out to her from downstairs.

"Coming." Lilac went down the steps.

"What are you doing here?"

"I came to see you." Nardo replied.

Ruby invited him in, closed the front door and walked off into the kitchen.

"You can have a seat."

Lilac sat down on one of two bean chairs and Nardo joined her on the other. Sweeper plopped down on the hardwood floor near the kitchen.

"What type of dog is he?" Lilac asked.

"Afghan hound," said Nardo.

Lilac sighed. "You totally blew me off at lunch. Why are you here?"

"I was still reeling about the rejection hotline incident."

"You have to admit, it was funny though."

"No it wasn't. That was such a cruel thing to do."

"I'm sorry."

Nardo's lips twisted up into a half-smile. "Apology accepted."

"Now that we've got that out of the way, I'd like to show you something?"

"Sure." Nardo got up.

"Mom, is it okay if Nardo and I go to my room?"

"What on earth for?"

"I'd like to show him my collection."

"All right, but be respectful."

"Yes Ma'am," Lilac said, rolling her eyes.

They left the living room, walked up the steps that were lined with linoleum and entered her room near the top of the stairs. A light green shag carpet brushed against Nardo's shoes as he entered the room with peach walls.

"What are they?" Nardo pointed to the pictures on her wall.

"They're pictures of the people who have bullied me over the years."

"Really?"

"Yup, I figured since I couldn't harm them physically, I'd illustrate the ways I'd like to exact my revenge."

One of the drawings depicted a girl with her ponytails cut off. Lilac stood above her with the scissors. Another showed a guy strung up to a tree by his balls. A hard gulp slid down Nardo's throat. *Yikes*! Nardo's hands edged closer to his groin.

"Anyway," Lilac reached into a tank on a side table near her bed. "This is my turtle, Oscar. You've already met Sugar."

"What is this?" He picked up one of her dolls.

"It's a worry doll. I've been working on it for years. The other dolls pinned to the walls are hex dolls."

"You have a gift for doll-making."

"Thanks."

He sat on her bed and patted the space beside him. "Sit with me?"

She sat near him.

"I have a question."

"I'm listening."

"Why did you give me the wrong number?"

"I thought you were collecting numbers."

"I get where you're coming from but that's not the case. Um…"

"What is it?"

"There will be a party later tonight. I know it's short notice but I'd like you to come. If you can't, it's okay."

She hesitated a moment. "I don't know."

"If you're worried about what other people will think, I'm not. Come with me. I promise we'll have a great time."

"What time does the party start?"

"9 PM."

"Okay, I'll go."

"Great. I got to go now, but I'll see you later." Nardo got up. Lilac followed him downstairs and they walked toward the front door.

Ruby walked out of the kitchen, "You're leaving already?"

"Yes, I can't stay. Thank you for welcoming me into your home."

"You're welcome." Sweeper got up from his post near the kitchen and followed Nardo outside.

* * *

Nardo took his time walking home. The moon was coy tonight; it hid behind a slew of thick clouds. He cut through an alley that led to a series of garages. Three

34

boys stepped out of the shadows, and one of them who was directly in front of Nardo flipped out a blade.

"What's your name?"

Nardo put his hands up. "I don't want any trouble."

"I said, what's your name?"

"Nardo." He could hear his mom already. *Shortcuts lead to destruction, stay out of dark alleys,* she told him countless times before, but does any teenager ever listen to their parents? Now he wished he had listened. Sweeper looked up at Nardo, then at the boys.

Nardo shook his head. "Sweeper you're useless."

"What did you say?" Dark eyes glared at him through a three hole knit ski mask over the face of a tall fellow with medium-sized man boobs and a hearty fold of fat over his belt. He pushed up against Nardo.

"I was talking to my dog, Sweeper." His breaths shortened.

"Just smell him and let's get this over with." A clear plastic mask clung to the face of the short muscular one and sweat drenched his white shirt. He eased in taking in Nardo's odor.

Nardo's eyebrows bunched, "What's going on?"

"He's clean. Let him go."

They walked away, but it took Nardo a minute to catch his breath and stop shaking. He ran home with Sweeper on his tail. Nardo slowed down as he approached his house. He walked to the porch and sat on the steps. Sweeper panted as he drank from his water bowl on the porch. Nardo took quick deep breaths and went inside.

His mother looked at him. "Are you okay?"

"I'm fine. I'm just tired."

He went upstairs and took a shower. Nardo closed his eyes and pressed his hand against the mauve-colored tiles as the cool water ran over his head. He couldn't phantom why his scent would matter to a bunch of thugs. He got out of the shower and wrapped a towel around his waist. Nardo wiped the mist off the large ornate mirror with a hand towel and cocked his head. There were hairs sprouting from his chin.

Nardo went to his room, and flicked on the light. The dark blue walls came alive with the posters of race cars and female wrestlers. He got dressed, went downstairs, and picked up a thick phone book off the accent table. He flipped through it until he came across a section of people whose last names began with *p*. Paine, Ruby was at the top of the list. He copied down the number.

Nardo smirked, "I have you now." He dialed.

"Hello."

"Good evening, may I speak to Lilac, please?"

"Who's calling?"

"It's Nardo, I was there earlier."

"Yes, hold on."

"Hello."

"Hi, I wanted to talk to you before the party."

"We just talked thirty minutes ago. Wait a minute, how did you get my number?"

"The phone book."

Lilac sighed. "I'm having second thoughts."

"Don't say that. You'll be fine."

The phone line went silent. They listened to each other breathing for a while.

"Nardo?"

"Hmm." He laid on his bed looking up at the ceiling filled with glowing stars. "Thanks for being nice to me even when I didn't deserve it."

"I'm going to eat dinner now, but I'll see you in a few hours; bye."

Lilac put the phone down. She tried to conceal her excitement, but in the matter of a few seconds, she had pranced around the room quietly squealing and flopped on her bed. She calmed herself and went downstairs to get a bite to eat. Lilac cut through her dinner like a mower and got up from the table.

Ruby's eyes widened. "That's the fastest I've ever seen you eat."

"Nardo will be here soon."

Ruby smirked, "Okay."

Lilac went upstairs, got dressed and fixed her hair. She slipped inside her mother's bedroom, sprayed on one of her perfumes and went downstairs. The soft light in the staircase shone on her as she walked downstairs in a pink and grey tie dye tank top paired with grey skinny jeans and was sporting a rare smile.

"You look adorable." Ruby hugged her. "And you smell good too."

"Thanks Mom." Lilac went out the front door and waited for Nardo on the porch. She saw the broad headlights coming down Zephyr Street. Nardo parked in front of her house. He stepped out of a red 2040 Oldsmobile Cutlass Supreme Convertible. She walked down the steps and he opened the passenger door.

"What happened to your bike?"

She sat on the cream leather seats as he closed the door.

"Nothing. It's at home. I borrowed my dad's car. I thought it would be more appropriate for the occasion."

He pulled away from her residence and drove down the street. They arrived at the party a short time later. There were a lot of people there and eighty percent of them were dancing, but it soon morphed into dirty dancing. Nardo held her hand as they moved through the crowd. He saw his friends, loosened his grip on Lilac's hand and went over to them. He gave Renaldo a charismatic hand slap followed by a couple of quick hand moves.

"How's it going?"

"All right, I guess. The weirdest thing happened to me earlier."

"What happened?"

"Three guys stopped me in the alley on my way home." Nardo shook his head and exhaled.

"So what did they want?"

"The hell if I know. One of them smelled me. I was worried it was going to end badly but they let me go."

"That's some weird shit. Maybe they were sweet on you." Renaldo burst out laughing.

"It's not funny, dude." His jaw hardened.

"Take it easy, Bro. I'm just bugging you. Have a beer." He pressed a cold one to Nardo's hand.

"I'll pass on that."

"Come on, let's go play some pool in the basement. The rest of the team's down there."

Renaldo and Nardo sifted through the partygoers and went down the basement stairs. Lilac was left to mingle amongst strangers that were pressed against the wall. Smoke chimed from a sofa a few feet away where two guys toked on a *spliff* and passed it back and forth to each other. When they weren't smoking, they were munching on a pile of cookies. Lilac sifted through a clearing until she found the bathroom.

It was the only place she could avoid their stares, the erratic dancing, and the stench of weed. She pulled out a can of shoe polish from her bag and applied it as eye shadow. *I don't care what people think. Why should I spend five to seven dollars on eye shadow when I can get shoe polish for a buck at the dollar store?* She thought. Someone knocked on the door.

"I'll be right out."

She opened the door and took in the figure before her. A tall guy with short blond hair stood before her.

"I don't mean to rush you, but someone spilled grape juice on me."

Lilac almost didn't hear him. She was too busy admiring his eyes; they were the bluest she'd ever seen.

"It's okay, I'm finished." She edged around him. *I'd wouldn't mind helping you get out the stain.*

"Thanks. What's your name?"

"Lilac."

"And yours?"

"Oliver. So tell me, how do I get this stain out?"

Lilac's mouth gaped. *Wishes do come true.* "I can use my Tide-To-Go Stain pen." Lilac pulled it out of a side pocket of her purse.

"You're resourceful." A slight smile appeared on his face. "So do I take the shirt off or leave it on?"

A devilish smile appeared on Lilac's face. "Take it off."

He entered the bathroom and shrugged his shirt over his head displaying his well-defined chest. Her eyes traveled to his pecs and she gulped. She took the shirt and slipped her hand through it, rubbed the *Tide To Go* pen on the stain and the stain disappeared. Lilac turned the shirt back to the right side and gave it to him.

The buzz of the party chimed behind him as they stared awkwardly at one another for a hot second. Nardo walked by the open door looking from side to side. He looked in the bathroom and saw Lilac in the bathroom with a shirtless guy.

Oliver put on his shirt. "You're a miracle worker."

"Thank you." Lilac's face lit up in admiration.

"Has anyone ever told you how cute you are?"

40

"No."

Nardo grimaced. His heart shrank to the size of a peanut. He told her that she was pretty plenty of times or maybe he never got around to it. He walked away. Lilac jerked to attention when she saw Nardo walking away. She didn't see him again until the party was over. He was sitting next to the two guys choked in a cloud of smoke. She walked over to him.

"Hey Nardo, are you ready to go?"

"I was ready twenty minutes ago. Let's go." He got up and walked to the entrance; Lilac followed. There was an uncomfortable silence between them during the ride home.

Lilac couldn't stand the silence any longer. "Did you have fun?"

"The party was great." His face was expressionless.

"You don't look like you had a great time. Where'd you go anyway?"

"I was around. I didn't know where to find you."

His face continued to sour.

"Is something wrong?" *What does he mean he couldn't find me? He's the one who left me alone at the party, the jerk.*

He turned the radio up. She didn't say a word after that.

* * *

Nardo parked in front of her house and got out to open the door for Lilac but she got out first and walked away. Nardo kicked a pebble across the pavement, got back in

41

the car and drove away. Lilac went inside, threw her jacket on the couch and flopped down on the chair.

Ruby walked into the living room. "How was the party?"

"He ditched me within the first ten minutes." Lilac sulked.

"That's not smart."

"I agree, but when one door closes another opens." Lilac pursed her lips.

"I met someone and he gave me his number. Do you think I should call?"

"Boys are strange. You should wait for him to call you."

"Thanks. I'm going to bed. Goodnight."

"Wait a minute. I made some seaweed and lime puree body scrub. Would you like to try it?"

Lilac took the mason jar from her mother. "Thank you. I'll try it. I haven't exfoliated in weeks."
She went upstairs to the bathroom and filled the tub with water. Lilac undressed and stepped into the tub. She applied the scrub to her body.

"Mom this is great!" She shouted.

"I'm glad you like it. I'm going to bed now, good night." Ruby walked past the bathroom down the hall to her bedroom and closed her door.

Lilac rinsed off and got out. She put on her pajamas and was about to get into bed but instead, she walked down the hall to her mom's room and knocked on her door.

Ruby sat up in the bed. "Come in."

"Can you tell me a bedtime story?"

Ruby laughed, "You're sixteen years old. Don't you think you're too old for that?"

"No. You're never too old to snuggle up to your mother while she tells you a good story."

"That's true." Ruby lifted the sheets and Lilac got in bed with her.

FOUR

Lilac woke the next day knowing that she'd have to do her least favorite thing, read in front of the class. She dreaded going to Mr. Peebles class. He had the shoulders of a linebacker and a head that looked like it had been shrink-wrapped for decades. The students often joked that he had escaped from a head shrinking clan. If that was truly the case, she hoped that they would find him and finish the job. It seemed to her that he enjoyed making her life miserable.

For each assignment that she was a part of, he always called her first or second. Despite his indiscretion, Lilac liked his class today. This time, three students had already spoken. *Finally, she wasn't first or second. Maybe he didn't have it in for her after all.*

"Who's up next?" Mr. Peebles's eyes traveled the room.

"Lilac hasn't gone yet." A smirk trailed on Sami's face.

Her curly red hair hugged her slim face. Lilac shot a nasty glare at her and she grinned back. Lilac managed to keep her angst in check. The last thing she wanted to do was morph, which tended to happen when she was angry. Sami was always ousting someone. She was the equivalent of the town crier and once she got wind of anyone's business it would be all over the school.

Lilac walked to the front of the class. Everything was a blur after that. She didn't even remember talking, but it was soon over and she returned to her seat.

"Thank you for sharing that Shakespearian verse with us." Lilac walked to her desk and sat down.

Mr. Peebles let out a heavy sigh. "Who's next?" The students' presentation continued for the remainder of class until the bell rang.

"I'll see you all tomorrow." He erased the blackboard.

Lilac walked into the hall. She looked at the clock on the wall and then fought her way through the crowd as book bags bumped her chest and back. Lilac made it to the main office. Ruby sat outside the office in the waiting area.

"Hi, Mom."

"Hi." She got up, entered the office and walked to the secretary's desk. "She'll be leaving early today for a dental appointment."

The secretary looked up from a novel she was reading. "You'll have to sign her out for the day on the clipboard." Ruby signed the paper and they left the office.

"Can we get a bite to eat afterward? There's a Big Mac with my name on it somewhere."

Ruby chuckled. "Sure we can do that too."

She pulled up and parked outside the dentist's office. Lilac got out of the car. Ruby saw that familiar look on Lilac's face. "Come on, let's go inside."

Lilac sat in the hygienists' chair. She kept moving her mouth and adjusting her head. Lilac didn't seem interested in making the hygienists' job easy. She couldn't help thinking that she'd rather mow an entire golf course than go to the dentist, but her mother was adamant about her maintaining perfect teeth. She left the dentist's office twenty minutes later agitated, but at least she had sparkling white teeth. Ruby beamed from her accomplishment.

"You have no cavities so that's a reason to smile."

Lilac groaned and forced a smile that quickly faded. "I suppose."

Ruby drove down the slope to a green light ahead. An ambulance siren tickled her eardrums, and got louder by the second. It cut Ruby off as it shot out of the other end of the crossroad and made a hard right turn. Ruby's tires screeched to a stop and it sent her and Lilac's upper body jolting toward the dashboard. A slew of police cars followed and they all parked down the street.

"My goodness, they damn near killed us." Their hearts rattled like crazed animals tugging on a cage.

"Are you okay?"

"I'm fine, Mom."

"I wonder what's going on down there."

The street ahead was choked with police cars and cordoned off with police tape. Ruby took another route. She kept her promise and took Lilac to get a burger. They got home a short time later, pulled into the garage and went inside. Lilac took the last bite of her Big Mac, went

46

into the living room and turned on the TV. A breaking news headline cut into a talk show segment.

"Good afternoon. I'm Barbara Tanner reporting for Channel 13 News. It appears that there is a crime scene downtown.

We have reporter, Maureen Chandler on the corner of Palmer Street in the historic district of downtown Charleston, Oregon, with an eye witness that may shed some light on what's going on."

"Good afternoon, I'm, Maureen Chandler reporting from Palmer's Street, the road that connects with Glen Street downtown. I'm here with Clifford Stokes, a resident of Kipling Apartments located directly across from the scene." A tall lanky white male with a greasy five o'clock shadow, a white tank top and polyester slacks palmed his chin.

"Clifford, could you tell us what you saw on the scene?"

"I was sitting on the porch of my first floor apartment with my grandson when I saw a tribe of cops coming to the scene. This is a quiet neighborhood. The last thing I expected to see was body after body being wheeled out."

"Can you tell us how many bodies have been removed?"

"I don't know; there were quite a few."

"Thank you for sharing your account with us."

"You're welcome. I hope that whatever happened here is resolved, because it's at my front door and that's scary."

"We will continue to keep you informed when more information becomes available. I'm Maureen Chandler reporting for Channel 13 News."

"Now we'll go back to Barbara Tanner in the news room."

Lilac changed the channel, but every channel was discussing the incident. During times like these, she wished that they had cable. Ruby put Silence of the Lambs in the movie player.

"Lilac, would you like to invite your friend over?"

"Sure, I'll text Nardo."

Fifteen minutes later, they heard a knock at the front door and Lilac answered.

"Hi, Lilac."

"Come in and make yourself at home."

They went into the living room and Ruby went into the kitchen.

Nardo looked at Lilac. "I'm sorry for leaving you alone at the party. It was a rude and insensitive thing to do. I swear it wasn't intentional."

Her mom was right; *boys are weird.* "You're forgiven."

"I have something for you." Nardo smiled from ear to ear. "I hope you like it."

"What is it?"

He took a green jewelry box decorated with gold sparkles with a lock at the opening out of his pocket. Nardo gave her the box. A smile grew on her face. She had never gotten a present from a guy before, except for the gifts she got from her dad when she was little. Her heart fluttered and her cheeks went from a pale white to a fiery red.

"How do I open it?"

"Pull the lock."

Lilac opened it. Inside was a silver necklace with a flower pendant.

"It's a lilac flower." Her eyes welled up.

"Can you put it on for me?"

"Sure."

Lilac lifted her hair and Nardo put it on her. She stood before the mirror and ran her hand along the necklace.

"It's gorgeous. Thank you." Lilac turned around and kissed him on the cheek.

A knock on the door parted them. "I will get that." Lilac opened the door.

"Oliver, what are you doing here?"

"You forgot your stain remover pen on the bathroom sink. I was in the area and I saw your bike out front so I thought I would stop by and return it."

"Come in, were about to watch a movie." They went into the living room.

"Oliver, this is my friend, Nardo." They stared at each other and didn't say a word. The tension between them could choke an artichoke.

"You have a nice home, Lilac." The corners of Oliver's mouth gathered.

"Thank you."

"So what movie are we watching?" he asked.

"Silence of the Lambs. It's my favorite movie."
Ruby joined them with a tray of snacks and drinks. She placed it on the coffee table.

"Mom, this is Oliver. The guy I told you about."

"Nice to meet you, Oliver."

Ruby sat between Oliver and Nardo. "Start the movie."

They spent an hour-and-a-half watching the movie in complete silence. The diabolical nature of the good doctor left them reeling with fear. Finally, the movie was over.

Nardo pulled Lilac aside, "What is he doing here?"

"I am not a translator. You were there when he explained."
Nardo huffed. "It's pretty obvious. He likes you. I should go."

"Don't be silly, stay a while."

"Okay." He made himself comfortable.

Lilac switched to TV mode and turned the channel to *I love Lucy*. Nardo looked at Oliver at the corner of his eye. He grimaced and put a glass to his lips.

Oliver got up. "This was fun, but I have to get going."

Lilac escorted him to the front door. "Thank you for returning the stain stick. I didn't even realize I forgot it."

"You're welcome. I'll see you around." Oliver left.

Nardo got up. "I'll be back." He followed Oliver out the front door.

"Hey Oliver, wait up. Can I ask you a question?"

"What is it?"

"Do you like Lilac?"

"No, she's not my type. I can be friends with her, but I wouldn't date her."

"I don't blame you. She's kind of weird."

"You're sweet on her aren't you?"

"I think she's beautiful and her weirdness is what makes me like her even more but I can't tell her that."

"Good luck with that." Oliver walked away. Nardo made his way back and by then Lilac was sitting outside on the steps, looking out at the skyline. Nardo walked to her and sat next to her.

What was that about?"

"We were talking about guy stuff. It's getting late; I should go. I'll see you tomorrow."

"Thank you for the necklace. It's pretty." Lilac said, touching the necklace lightly.

"I'm glad you like it." Nardo got on his bike and drove away feeling like he'd done something miraculous, like he'd touched a special place in her heart.

FIVE

That night when he got home, his mind wandered into places that left him open to many possibilities. Nardo called Lilac when he woke up the next day.

"Would you like to hang out with me at the park? You can bring Sugar if you like."

"Sure, I don't have anything planned. What time?"

"I can meet you there at 11 AM."

She arrived at the park and saw Nardo with Sweeper in tow. The park was filled with dog walkers and children keen on getting a full day of play in. Lilac decided to bring Oscar along instead. Sugar was always wandering off somewhere and she wasn't in the mood for that.

"Hi." He noticed Lilac had her turtle, Oscar, in a stroller. He crawled around on a plush blanket.

"Can I ask you something?"

"Sure, go ahead."

"What type of guy do you like?"

"Why do you want to know?"

"I'm just curious."

"I don't have a type."

"Everyone has a type. My ideal girl would be pretty with long hair and exotic eyes. She'd be smart, love sports but not all of them, and she doesn't have to be normal."

"I thought you were going to say that she has to be a Brazilian like you, but I like your answer better," she said with a grin.

"I don't discriminate. Let's go get some ice cream. There's a parlor across the street."

"Let's go then," Lilac said.

They crossed the street and walked to the ice cream shop. Nardo stopped at the entrance. He noticed a sticker on the door. *No Pets allowed.* "I'll buy our ice cream."

"I'll keep an eye on them. Get me a pumpkin flavor, please."

Nardo came out with the cones in hand. Lilac took hers.

"So where do we go from here?"

"Isn't your house near here, Nardo?"

"It's a block away."

"Come on, let's go." She held on to his arm.

They took a short stroll to his house. Nardo opened his front door, "Mom, I brought a friend."

"Who's your friend?" Rosita stood near the kitchen. Her petite face and long straight blonde hair flowed past her shoulders.

"This is Lilac. She goes to my school."

"Nice to meet you. Is she your girlfriend?"

"Yes, isn't she just gorgeous?"

Lilac elbowed him in the side. "I'm not your girlfriend." Lilac spoke in a whisper.

"She's a pretty one. You have good taste."

"Thank you, Mrs. Aguilar," Lilac replied awkwardly.

"We're about to have lunch. Go get your father, he's in the garage."

"Dad, lunch is ready." Nardo shouted from a side door.

A tall stocky man with curly brown hair came in the kitchen. "What's for lunch?"

"Have a seat; the food is coming," Nardo's mom brought plates of food out to the table.

"We have a guest. This is Lilac, Nardo's girlfriend."

Lilac kicked Nardo in the shin.

"Ouch." Nardo's parent's looked at him.

"Is everything all right?"

"Yes."

"It's nice to meet you, Lilac." They began eating the tamales she'd prepared.

"How'd you two meet?"

"In gym class."

"Do you play lacrosse?" Bernie asked.

"No, but the girls had to learn the game." Lilac finished her tamales in a few bites.

"Is it okay if we go to my room?"

"Sure but keep it kosher." Mr. Aguilar spoke in a stern tone.

"Let's go," Nardo suggested.
They walked down the hall.

"Your parents are nice."

"Thanks."

"Why did you tell them I was your girlfriend?"

"I was just joking around. My mom's always asking, so I figured if I told her you were my girlfriend she'd stop asking."

Lilac's head lowered and a tear streamed down her cheek.

"Why are you crying? I didn't mean to upset you with the girlfriend thing." He wiped her tear away.

"It's not that. Seeing you with your family reminded me of when my dad was alive."

He pulled Lilac into his arms and stroked the back of her hair. "I'm sorry. I didn't know."

Now tears streaked down her cheeks, leaving a lick of salt.

"Pretty girls shouldn't cry."

Her head lay against his chest. "You think I'm pretty?"

"No. I think you're beautiful."

Lilac blushed through her tears.

"I want to show you something."

She watched as Nardo looked through his bookshelf and pulled out an album. "Have a seat." They sat at the edge of his bed. He opened the album and flipped through it as Lilac looked at the photos.

"Now tell me. Don't I look sexy?" Nardo pointed to a baby picture of him fresh out of the bath.

Lilac giggled, "Oh my goodness your noodle is showing."

He laughed, "That's how real men take pictures." Nardo chuckled.

"You're a nut, but an adorable one."

Lilac yawned. "You look tired. You can lie on my bed if you want."

"Can you keep an eye on Oscar?"

"I can handle it."

She crawled under the covers and Nardo lay on top of the sheet next to her. She elbowed him, "No cuddling allowed."

Lilac fell asleep and Nardo snuck under the covers beside her. In no time, he fell asleep too. She woke a half-hour later, passed her hand along Nardo's cheek, and traced her fingers on his lips. *He's perfect. Too perfect for me.* Lilac got off the bed, got Oscar and left.

SIX

Lilac walked through the hall. A girl skipped by her and twirled clutching a box of chocolates. Lilac eased around her and entered the cafeteria. A group of girls crowded around Nardo with boxes of chocolate and roses. Lilac shoulders slumped; she looked down at the box in her hand and sat on a vacant seat at a corner table. She watched as Nardo packed boxes of chocolates in a large green gift bag. He walked over to her.

"Happy Valentine's Day."

"Happy Valentine's Day." She dragged her words.

"You've got chocolate."

She tucked the chocolates behind her back and lowered her eyes. "What do you care?"

"I do care. Why are you so antsy?"

"No particular reason."

"I guess Oliver liked you more than he let on."

"Did Oliver say something to you?"

"Yes, he did." Envy grew on Nardo's face like weeds.

"You're acting as if it was impossible for him to like me. After all, you said that I was beautiful so someone else had to notice too."

"Remind me to kick myself." Nardo walked away.
Lilac threw the box of chocolates on the floor and left.

Nardo heard something tumble to the floor and looked back. He saw the box on the floor, walked back to it and picked it up. He read the tag. From: Lilac To: Nardo.

* * *

Lilac called Oliver when she got home from school. They made arrangements to meet at the Sweet Treat Deli. When she arrived at the shop, he was already there. She walked over and sat down.

"Have you been waiting long?"

"No I got here a few minutes ago."

"Can I ask you something?"

"Sure, what is it?"

"Do you like me?"

"Of course I do. I even told your friend, Nardo, that I liked you."

"He never mentioned it until today."

"Isn't it obvious?" Oliver asked.

"What is?"

"He likes you a lot. You're blind if you can't see that. Guys rarely talk about their feelings. That's a girl thing to do."

"I have to go. I'll talk to you another time." Lilac hurried through the door, got on her scooter and putted away. Light hail fell from the sky and bounced off of her. She heard stories about the past and what it was like back then but to her it was a foreign concept. All she knew was the world she lived in. Lilac grimaced beneath her helmet.

The clear skies of decades past were no more. Daylight was accompanied by the unyielding beauty of *aurora borealis* that left a superfluous rainbow haze in the sky. The sun and moon illuminated the strange world in which they lived but nature had formed its own rebellion. They'd intruded on the fabric that made their world unique and now the earth had exacted its revenge.

She drove down Zephyr Street and parked outside her home. Lilac glanced at the eyesore next door and gasped. *Helena, what is she doing over there*? A flood of memories came to her. The moments they'd spent together and all of the strange things she'd shown her over the years. Lilac took off her helmet and walked to the steps. Nardo had been waiting for the past twenty minutes. He walked down the steps and stood in front of her.

"We need to talk." He studied her face. "Is something wrong?"

Lilac's breaths sounded a bit off. "I need to sit down." He held her hand and a cold chill shot up his arm. She sat on the wicker chair and he stood in front of her.

"What's wrong?" Lilac stared at the house across the street.

"If there was anything I did to hurt you or make you mad at me, I'm sorry." Nardo pulled a bouquet of carnations from behind his back.

She glared at him, got up and walked to the front door.

"I can't win with you no matter what I do."

Lilac turned to him. "I never imagine that the only friend I had left would lie to me or rob me of a chance at happiness."

"What are you talking about?"

"You lied to me."

"I have no idea what you're talking about. You've drawn your own conclusions and I'll do the same." His jaw line hardened.

"You didn't tell me that Oliver liked me."

"That's not what he told me. Besides, I didn't think you cared to know."

"Of course I care."

"I asked Oliver if he liked you because I can't seem to get you out of my mind," Nardo confessed. Lilac looked away.

"I'm flattered, but I'm easy to forget."

"I disagree. You have some kind of freakish hold on me. Before I forget, thanks for the chocolates. I didn't want to hurt their feelings so I accepted the chocolates from the other girls."

Lilac looked at him sideways.

"I don't care that you eat bugs, smell like blue cheese on a bad day or morph out when you're pissed. I can't help liking you. Aren't you going to say anything?"

"Can I tell you something?"

"I'm all ears."

"I'm upset, but not for the reason you think."

Ruby opened the front door and stuck her head out.

"Hi, Mom."

60

"Good afternoon, Mrs. Paine."

"Hi, Nardo. Would you like something to drink?"

"Yes, please."

Nardo turned to Lilac. "What's on your mind?" They sat down.

"When I came home, I saw someone I met when I was five."

Nardo reached over and tucked her hair behind her earlobes. "I meant what I said; I can't seem to get you off my mind."

Her heart raced as she looked at him. "I don't know what to say."

Ruby came out with two glasses of water full of ice that chimed as it gathered at the rim of the glasses.

"You don't have to say anything. My mom's probably wondering where I am; I should go. You can call me later if you'd like."

"Good night." Lilac watched Nardo drive away. She went inside, sat next to her mom in the living room and rested her head on her shoulder.

"Is everything okay?"

"Yes."

"All right but I'm here if you need me."

"I know." Lilac kissed her mother on the cheek and went upstairs to her room.

She crawled out of her window and rested her back against the grainy shingles on the roof. Lilac stared at the blotchy yellow-colored moon and looked next door at the house that had been vacant for as long as she could remember. Before they bought their home, they'd lived in an apartment and then they moved to their beautiful two story cream house with a red roof and white picket fence.

Unfortunately, there were no kids her age, but that changed when Helena started coming around. She would watch Lilac from a distance, but once she got used to her, she introduced herself. Helena wasn't the best at communicating, but she did her best to get her point across.

Back then, the house was a beautiful uninhabited splendor. She'd never entered its walls, but she had an unexplainable familiarity with the property. As the years past, the paint faded, weeds grew out of the spouting and the lawn looked like it caught an incurable case of mange. The neighbors grumbled to one another, but no one cared enough to do more beyond that.

At one point, her father, Kent, had a wild idea to buy the property, fix it up and rent it out. Anything was better than what the home came to symbolize. He'd promised that summer to follow through with his plans. Her parent's discussed it on the road trip to grandma's house.

To her, summertime in Nevada was magical. The eleven hour drive was filled with every emotion known to man but it was well worth seeing her maternal grandmother, Vivian Chancellor. The last time she saw her, Lilac sat near her grandmother's feet while she sat in her favorite chair. Lilac stared at her beautiful hazel eyes and shiny gray hair. Her eyelashes amazed Lilac. They seemed to go on forever. When she put that black stuff on them, her eyelashes made her eyes look even more beautiful. Lilac eased her way onto Vivian's lap and traced her tiny finger along the lines on her face. "Grandma, why do you have so many lines?"

Vivian smiled. "My daddy use to say, 'God gives us wrinkles to mark the journey. You only get them when you've truly lived.'"

"Really?" Lilac beamed. "I can't wait to get some." Vivian burst into a hearty laugh. "You'll have plenty of time for that." Vivian hugged and kissed her on the cheek. It was one of Lilac's fondest memories.

The dull thud of the tires gripping the unforgiving road as cars whisked by filled the moments that group songs failed to shorten. She'd familiarized herself with landmarks that signaled that grandma's house was near. They passed the large water tower and she sighed. Lilac reached for her book, *Where The Wild Things Are* and flipped open to the first page. The illustrations held her imagination, temporarily releasing her from the back seat of the car. Ruby and Kent engaged in meaningful chatter, but to her it translated into incoherent babble.

Their minivan traveled around a two-way curve separated by concrete dividers. Lines of cars swooped the curve at ease. A big rig, banking the curve on the westbound lane, shifted its load, sending the trailer toppling to the side. A continuous roll followed and it tumbled into the divider. The rig pushed and crushed everything in its path. The Paine's blue Honda minivan was partially crushed on the driver's side, pinning the right side of Kent's body. The rest of the car had folded like an accordion and Lilac and Ruby were trapped.

Lilac was barely seven at the time, but she remembered it like it was yesterday. It's strange how a split second can change your life. It devastated their family and forever changed their lives. Vivian was there for Lilac and Ruby throughout their recovery, which lasted a year. When they had fully recovered from their injuries, they returned to Oregon. Vivian gained more lines and she died a month later. Ruby had said, 'she lived long enough to see us through the storm.' Lilac couldn't believe how much time had passed. Tomorrow would be the tenth anniversary of her father's death, but it still hurt as if he died yesterday.

* * *

Ruby and Lilac drove to the cemetery to pay their respects. Tears accumulated at the side of Ruby's jawline. After she parked, they walked through the grass to his plot and stood near his tombstone.

A lone tear rolled down her cheek. "I love you Dad." Every time they visited the cemetery, Lilac found herself reliving the funeral all over again. The church filled with loved ones, her being pushed in her wheelchair to the open casket and placing a single rose on top of her father's chest. They sang Amazing Grace but he would have preferred, The Unchained Melody by The Righteous Brothers. He would have wanted his last day with them to bring a faint smile to their face even during one of the most painful days of their lives.

Ruby sat in the front pew sobbing in the arms of her younger sister, Roma. She was an anomaly. Ruby always said Roma reminded her of *Lourdes Chacon*, a Puerto Rican singer and dancer from the 70s, but Roma's hair was red. Roma was a burlesque dancer in Las Vegas but once she'd heard of the accident, she dropped everything and came to Nevada. They knew it was Roma when she entered their hospital room; she smelled like a perfumery. Tight Jordache jeans hugged her curvy hips. She wore a full shirt with a belt at the waist, and stilettoes. Her voluminous hair was hair-sprayed to perfection. Despite her bold look, Roma had a way of making people feel like they were the most important person in a room. Lilac looked at Ruby; she'd aged so much since then.

"Your father was a good man." Ruby rubbed Lilac's back.

"I know. I miss him so much." She hugged Lilac and kissed the top of her head.

Lilac saw Helena as she looked up. She'd always made a point of being there when Lilac was sad. Perhaps it was time for her to return the favor. She watched Helena walk away.

"Is something wrong?" Ruby turned to look but Helena was already gone.

Lilac wished her mother could understand how important Helena was to her but she hadn't. Instead, she did everything in her power to keep them apart. She thought Helena was a bad influence, but she wasn't. She was her best friend. Mentioning her name made Ruby angry, so Lilac pretended like everything was fine. Over the years, Ruby began to feel that Helena's hold on her was finally over.

* * *

They left the Kingshill Cemetery and drove through town. Lilac stared through the window looking at the buildings blur as her mother whisked by. They didn't say much on the ride home; the sounds of nature and life in motion took over. Ruby pulled into the garage and they went inside. Lilac turned on the TV and flipped through the channels. She stopped on the evening news.

"Mom the news is on."

Ruby came out of the kitchen and she sat next to her.

"Turn up the volume."

Lilac grabbed the remote off the living room table and adjusted the volume.

*"**I'm Maureen Chandler reporting for Channel 13 News. A body was found at the Kingshill Cemetery this afternoon**."*

"I can't watch this. I've dealt with enough gloom and doom for the day. I'm going to get ready."

"For what?"

"I'm going to the Drive-In Theater with Nardo." Lilac went upstairs to her room, and peered in the mirror. She applied blue lipstick and fluffed her hair. Ruby walked up behind her and they put their faces side by side.

"What do you think?"

Ruby looked at Lilac. "I like it."

"I have to go. I don't want to keep him waiting."

"Is he picking you up?"

"He didn't ask me if I wanted a ride."

"That was inconsiderate."

"Mom, please!"

"I'm trying to save you some heartache, but you're stubborn."

Lilac went downstairs and entered the garage. She adjusted the rear view mirrors that stuck out like butterfly antennas. She ran her hand against the tan leather seat brushing away dust that settled on it. Lilac pushed her bike out of the garage, climbed on her scooter and drove away. She zipped through the deserted streets and approached Nardo's house.

She soon pulled up in front of a banana-yellow home bordered by hedges and parked at the curb. Lilac walked up to the front door, and knocked. Nardo opened the door. "Come in," He said.

"Are we still going?" She asked, wondering why he invited her in the house.

"Yes, but I made a mess in the kitchen. We're leaving as soon as I'm done."

Lilac went to the living room and sat on the couch. Nardo went into the kitchen and cleaned up the mess he made. He grabbed his jacket and they left. They drove to the drive-in in his dad's convertible and parked in the middle of the field. The moon and sun both hovered high in the sky. The cool night air flowed around them as they looked at the movie screen. Nardo munched on his popcorn. "Lilac?"

She turned to him. "Yes."

"Would you like to be my girl?"

"Me?" Lilac laughed at the thought. Nardo slid closer and held her hand.

"Yes, you."

"Let me think about it and get back to you."

SEVEN

Lilac woke up early the next day in a cold sweat gasping for air. She looked out her window. She went downstairs and walked outside her front door. Lilac saw Nardo coming down the street. He stopped in front of her house.

"Were you going out?"

"Yes, I'm going next door. Come with me."

Nardo followed Lilac to the backyard where the Garner and Paine's fences met. She climbed the fence. Nardo helped her over and then climbed over himself. Lilac walked to the back door and turned the doorknob. "It's open."

"Someone must have left it unlocked," Nardo said.

"Keep an eye out just in case anyone sees us." Nardo looked around before he entered.

"What are you looking for? Whose house is this anyway?"

"The Garner's."

"Do you know them?"

"Not well, but If I tell you *how* I know them you'll think I'm crazy!"

"I already think you're weird so why would you care if I add crazy to the pile?" He chuckled.

Lilac turned the corner and went upstairs. "I don't care, but still it's hard to explain." Lilac stood at the top of the stairs.

She wasn't sure how long she'd been gone, but Helena's room was still in trend. She flipped through an old *American Girl* magazine. It gave her chills. It all makes sense now; Helena used to hover over her shoulder when Lilac read her American Girl magazine each month. She especially enjoyed working on the puzzles and questionnaires. Lilac sat on the bed and lifted the pillow; beneath it was a diary. She picked it up and read the inside of the cover: *This is the diary of Helena Garner.*

"Lilac, we should go."

"All right, I'm coming." They went down stairs.

"Shortly after we moved here, peculiar things started happening."

Lilac peered out the window at the garden behind their home that was filled with passionflowers sporting brilliant colors. "Helena started showing me things; things that terrified me. It got so bad that my parents took me to counseling. My therapist said it was triggered by the change of environment, but it wasn't that at all. I didn't like where we lived before, but I loved our new home here. My parents thought therapy would help. Then my dad died; the sessions helped me cope with his death. I was afraid that I had lost touch with reality."

"Were you close?"

"Yes, we were."

They left the Garner's house and climbed over the fence to her back yard. They entered Lilac's house through the back door and went upstairs to her room. They laid back on her bed as Lilac poured her heart out and Nardo listened to every word.

"For what it's worth, I believe you." Nardo got up on one elbow and gazed into her eyes. "I asked you a question more than a week ago and I'm still waiting for an answer."

Lilac looked away for a moment. *He must really like me if he is still interested after all that I've told him.* She returned his gaze. "I'd love to be your girlfriend." He held her close.

"That's great! So, what did you find?"

"A diary, but I almost feel like I shouldn't read it."

"Well, if it was important it wouldn't have been left behind."

Lilac opened Helena's diary. *Mother hasn't been herself ever since she started working on the case and sometimes I wonder if she even cares.* Lilac's head rose and she looked at Nardo.

"I feel like I'm invading her privacy." She closed the book. "I can't read it."

"It's getting late, I'll see you later." Nardo said, yawning.

Lilac walked him to the front door and waved at him as he left. She went back into the house. Ruby was fast asleep on their couch.

"Mom, wake up," Lilac shook her by the shoulder. "Wake up. I have something to show you."

Ruby's eyes edged opened.

"What?" Ruby murmured. "I wasn't making it up, and I have proof." Lilac gave her the diary and she read the inside of the front cover.

She looked at Lilac, "If this is a joke, I'm not laughing."

"I wouldn't lie about something that serious." Lilac walked into the kitchen and poured herself a glass of water.

"Where did you get it?"

"I found it in the house next door."

"Trespassing is against the law. You should know better than that."

"I know, but Helena came to me last night while I was asleep for the first time since I sent her away all those years ago. She pointed to the house. I couldn't ignore her any longer."

Ruby sighed. "I thought you were over her."

"How could I be over it when no one believed me?"

"All right I don't want to mull over the past. Just stay out of that house!"

"Fine!" Lilac ran upstairs sobbing.

* * *

Ruby turned on the TV.

"Good evening, I'm Barbara Tanner, reporting for Channel 13 News. Last week the body of a 9-year-old girl was found and some details have surfaced about what led to her death. The autopsy showed the young

72

girl died of asphyxiation. We also know the girl's identity. Her name is Helena Garner.

A missing children's report was never filed for her. The whereabouts of her parents are unknown, but those who knew them well might be able to shed light on the whereabouts of her family."

"If you have any information about her parent's whereabouts, please call 969-3333.

"Now, we'll go over to Albert King for the weather forecast."

Ruby looked at the diary. "Lilac!"

She came downstairs. "The girl they found in the cemetery is Helena."

"I told you I wasn't lying." Lilac ran upstairs to her room and closed the door.

Ruby stared at the TV for a while before she picked up the phone and made a call.

"I think I may have some information on the girl that was found."

An hour later, a tall slender officer with slick black hair walked up to their front door and rang the bell. Ruby answered the door.

"Hello, I'm Detective Baez. I'm here to take your statement."

"Come in."

She escorted him to the living room. "You can have a seat." He pulled a pad out of his pocket and sat down.

"How do you know the Garner family?"

"Well, I've never met them."

"I don't have time for games." He got up.

"Please, I'd like you to hear me out. There are some things that you should know."

He sighed and sat back down. "Okay," he shook his head. "I'm listening."

"That old house next door is where they use to live. We bought this house eleven years ago, but that house has been empty all this time. My husband and I were going to buy it at one point, but he passed away before we got around to it."

"I'm sorry for your loss."

"Thank you. Would you like a glass of lemonade?"

"Yes, please."

Ruby got up and went to the kitchen but continued talking. "About six months after we moved in, my daughter started mentioning Helena. When we asked her where she'd met her. She said, 'in my room.'" Ruby sighed. She gave the glass of lemonade to Officer Baez. "It was impossible. No one could get in this house without me knowing. Kent and I didn't think much of it. We just chalked it up to her imagination. When Kent died, it got worse. Each night, Lilac woke up gasping for breath as if someone was stifling her. When she caught her breath, she'd sob herself to sleep. In between her crying spells, she'd beg us to help Helena. We thought she was losing her mind, so we took her to see a therapist."

"She was diagnosed with paranoid schizophrenia, but it didn't make sense. I asked the doctor to hypnotize her.

It was clear that the therapist had misdiagnosed her. Lilac said the same things under hypnosis. I had no idea that Helena was real or that something awful happened to her."

"I'd like to speak with your daughter if that's okay with you?"

"Sure I'll get her. Lilac, could you come downstairs please?"

Lilac's feet dragged down the stairs and she sullenly walked into the living room.

"Officer Baez would like to ask you some questions about Helena." Lilac sat down.

"Has Helena ever mentioned if they were moving?"

"No, she didn't say anything about moving. If they were moving she would have told me."

"The last time she visited me before today was on my 13th birthday. I told her to go away. I was tired of being the loon on the block. I wanted to be normal."

"You are normal, Lilac. I should have told you long ago, but the last time I took you to your therapist, she hypnotized you. I learned that you weren't making things up. I thought that if I stopped taking you that you'd be fine, but I was wrong. I am so sorry."

Lilac burst into tears, "So you actually thought that letting me think that I was crazy was better?" Lilac glared at her.

Ruby felt bad before but now she felt really stupid.

"You told me I was seeing things." Lilac's voice went up an octave. "How could you?" Tears streamed down her face.

"I'm so sorry." Now Ruby was in tears too. "I hope you can forgive me. I thought I was doing the right thing."

Lilac couldn't bear to look at her. Ruby continued to talk but Lilac mentally blocked whatever she had to say. Ruby went to the kitchen and sobbed.

Lilac spent the next hour talking to Officer Baez. By the time he left, he was dumbfounded. He didn't know how he would avoid telling his superiors that the information came from a ghost that befriended a child. Officer Baez was apprehensive, but he had to do something. He left the Paine's residents and looked into getting information from Helena's school. Based on the records obtained from the school, they had proof of the last day she had attended. An autopsy was performed and it revealed the approximate time of death based on the food she ate at lunch. The digestive system is a good indicator of a victim's time of death. Digestion stops immediately upon death. It takes approximately six hours to digest food; there wasn't any food in her intestines. So she died within a matter of six hours after eating lunch at school.

Officer Baez contacted her parent's place of employment to get additional information on the duo. Sarah Garner worked as a staff writer for the local paper and Geoffrey Garner played a major role in scientific research. By all accounts, he wasn't given any reason to believe that they were bad parents. Neither of their employers had heard from either of them. Their employers thought it was odd that they hadn't shown up for work or called, but no one went the extra mile to contact the authorities.

Officer Baez was able to get a warrant, and the Garner's home was searched. Geoffrey's body was found in the shed, but Sarah was still unaccounted for.

EIGHT

Twelve years earlier, Helena grabbed her navy blue book bag and went downstairs. She got her lunch that her mother packed off the kitchen counter and walked to the bus stop. The bus pulled up before she got there so she ran to catch it. She arrived out of breath at the door just as the driver closed it. Helena knocked on the door.

Mrs. Rhymer, the bus driver, sat on a seat supported by springs. The folds of fat on her stomach hugged the bottom edge of the steering wheel. She glared at Helena as the door folded open.

"Time waits for no man or child!" She said and continued mumbling incoherently after that.

Helena sighed and got on the bus. She sat next to Amanda Tuttle. Amanda always put her bag in the empty seat next to her but moved her it so Helena could sit down. Amanda's mousey features made her an easy target for teasing, but Helena didn't care what she looked like. Amanda was kind and didn't have a mean bone in her body. Mrs. Rhymer drove ahead to pick up the next batch of students.

Shortly after Helena left for school, her mother got dressed and looked at her reflection in the mirror that hung over her dresser. Sarah trailed her finger along the edge of the dresser, filled with just about every perfume

Avon sold for the past 15 years. Half of them she hadn't used in over five years. It was the downside of being a former Avon representative. She made a mental note to dust later. Sarah grabbed her jacket and keys and went downstairs. She walked through a side door to the garage and put her files on the passenger seat of the car. A dry cracked old leather odor wafted through the 2024 Lincoln Continental. Sarah put the windows down and started the engine. A cloud of smoke came out of the exhaust.

Her husband poked his head inside of the garage. "I wish you'd let me buy you a new car. You wouldn't have to warm up anything. You'd just start the car and go."

"No, thank you. I can find better ways to spend your money." Sarah waved and backed out of the garage.

She had a twelve-hour shift ahead of her. Sarah had been working on an investigative report for the Charleston Daily Newspaper. After months of digging, she'd finally come across something that could shed light on her investigation. She'd been looking into the rise of incidents where residents were being confronted and harassed. Then a slew of missing person's reports were filed.

Geoffrey adjusted his tie and passed a comb through his thinning brown hair. Peering through his glasses, he saw specks of dust and water spots on the lens. He removed his glasses and cleaned them. His medical research had begun to consume his down time. All that mattered was the process and the results in his line of work. Lately, his research was going in an unexpected direction.

The day before, a fire broke out in the lab. A cleaning crew would be in today to clean up. He'd have to sort through what was left of his work. He got a quick bite to eat and went to work.

NINE

Geoffrey came home for lunch. He opened the front door and three masked men ambushed him as soon as he closed the door. They tied him up and questioned him. A man dressed in blue with quarter-sized gauges in his ears gave Geoffrey the phone.

"Call your wife and tell her to come home. Tell her whatever you have to, to get her here or else we'll kill you."

"I'll do what you ask."

Geoffrey called Sarah. His lips trembled as the man with the gauges pressed the phone to his ear while another with odd-colored eyes pointed a gun at him.

"I'm sorry to bother you at work but we have a busted pipe upstairs. I need you to come home."

"Sure I'll be right there." Yesterday he'd spent the better part of the morning trying to save what was left of his research and now they had a busted pipe upstairs.

"Thank you." He sighed. "I love you."

"I love you too Geoffrey. Is everything okay?"

"Everything's fine. Just come home." He ended the call.

Geoffrey closed his eyes and lowered his head. Another assailant paced in front of Geoffrey. A spider web tattoo covered the expanse of his broad neck. He went into the kitchen, took a knife out of the utensil tray and stabbed Geoffrey in the side of his neck.

Geoffrey gasped and held his neck. The chair tipped over and landed on its side. His head banged on the floor, sending the knife deeper into his carotid artery.

"That should teach you to stop playing God."

The man with the web tattoo and the other who had different color eyes untied Geoffrey, lifted his slim body and carried him out to the backyard. The man with the gauges opened the shed door and his 'join or die' tattoo of a dissected snake on his forearm went on display. His shirt hugged his muscular torso and was at least a size smaller than what he should have worn.

The other man dropped Geoffrey's body inside. He locked the door, put the padlock on, and buried the keys behind the shed. They went back to the kitchen and the man with the web tattoo washed his hands. Blood ran down the drain as it slipped off his hands. Sarah arrived fifteen minutes later. They grabbed her as soon as she entered the door.

"What's going on?"

"We have your husband. If you want to keep him alive, you'll do exactly as we say." A man with the two-toned eyes brandished a handgun in front of her.

"Come on were going for a ride." He grabbed Sarah by the arm and they walked through the kitchen to the garage. She noticed blood on the kitchen floor.

"Where's my husband?"

"He's out back. Cooperate and we won't harm him."

"I'll do whatever you need me to do. But please don't hurt him."

"You have my word. Let's go pick up your daughter from school."

"Why are we going—?"

"You're asking too many questions. Move it!"

They entered the garage and she got in the car. Two of them got into the back seat and the other sat in the front seat, pointing a gun at her. Sarah's blue Lincoln Continental backed out of the garage with the tinted windows up and drove away from Zephyr Street.

* * *

The phone in Helena's classroom rang. Mr. Figaro answered.

"Helena, pack up your things, please and go to the main office."

She gathered her belongings and walked to the office, wondering why she was called out. Then she saw her mother.

"Come on," her mom said, "I already signed you out."

They walked outside and over to her mom's car that was parked on the curve outside of the Kensington Elementary School office.

"Why do I have to leave early?"

"I have to go to Ledding County to work on a case and I won't be back until much later this evening."

"Can't I stay with dad?" Helena interjected.

Sarah hurried her along. "He'll be working late too."

Sarah's hands trembled as she entered the car and gripped the steering wheel. Helena looked in the back seat. Three men stared back at her and one of them had a gun pointed at her mother's back.

"Come on, let's go," the man with the gun said, and Sarah obediently pulled away from the curb.

The men whispered back and forth as she drove ahead.

"Where are we going?"

He wagged the pistol. "Take Route 9 to Lander's County."

"What about my husband? She begged for information.

"Don't worry about him. He's no longer an issue." He answered.

A hard gulp traveled down Sarah's throat, her breathing became faster and heavier and an uncontrollable chill shuddered through her body.

"Mom, I thought you said we were going to Ledding County."

"Yes, I did but, there has been a change of plans."

Sarah's eyes canvased their surroundings as they drove down Glen Street and drove toward Kingshill cemetery. She saw a green traffic light ahead that quickly turned yellow before she could get through. A car pulled up behind them. Sarah looked at Helena who looked as terrified as she felt. Just as the light turn red, she mouthed *run* without speaking. The light turned green and the car behind blasted its horn as their front doors flew open and they bolted from the car.

"Shit!" Two of the men ran after them. The other parked the car at the side of the road. The driver of the car behind them passed and blew his horn a few more times before driving away.

* * *

Sarah and Helena ran through the cemetery. The sodden grass brushed against the soles of their feet. The scent of decay was always present in the cemetery. Stagnant souls laid to rest in the earth played hide and seek with the living, envious of the oxygen enthused beings that visited their lair. We take life for granted while the dead wished that they could rewind time for a second chance at living.

Sarah stopped outside a mausoleum. "If they catch us they will hurt us. I want you to stay here. I'm going to lead them away but I'll be back to get you." She fumbled in her purse. "Here, you can use my flashlight." She kissed Helena and closed the mausoleum door.

Sarah ran across the lawn sobbing, trying to get as far away from her daughter as possible to keep her safe. The skies opened up and rain drenched her as she ran. The rain came down like there was no tomorrow, and in the matter of five minutes, a river of mud ran through the tombstones.

She saw the men running through a clearing amongst the headstones a short distance away; Sarah hid behind a cloaked statue. Water drenched her hair and ran down her face. It sent a shiver through her body. The men ran in the other direction; she doubled back and sprinted in the direction of her car. She ran swiftly as water splashed in the air up to her waist.

TEN

The worse part of looking for a missing loved one is not knowing what happened to them, but it appears that the Garner's had no immediate family. Fortunately, Helena had Lilac, and she had to figure out the rest. Lilac put the rest of the pieces together. She now knew what happened to Helena, and now she knew what happened to Sarah. Lilac picked up the phone and gave Officer Baez a call.

"Hello, this is Lilac Paine. I think I know where you can find Sarah Garner."

* * *

Sarah's breaths hastened as she ran ahead. One of the men spotted her and shouted to the others.

"She's over here!"

All three of them ran toward her. She looked around as she ran ahead. Sarah felt the ground beneath her give way and before she knew it, she became buried in it up to her waist. They walked up to her and watched as the water rushed into the freshly dug grave Sarah was standing in. She flapped her hands and clawed at the earth. "Help me!"

They just stood there, glaring. Water rushed up to her chest as her heart thumped frantically against her ribs. Water cascaded inside filling the grave in a hurry. Soon she found herself neck deep in muddy water and it gushed into her nose and ears until her nose was submerged. Sarah was never good at swimming or holding her breath, but now her life depended on it. There was no way she was going to die today. She tried to calm herself down and hold her breath, but it was hard to concentrate with the pressure building in her nose and ears. She gasped as water entered her mouth, choking her airway. Her body soon floated to the top and flipped over.

"Poor thing never had a chance." The spectators laughed and left, driving off in her Oldsmobile.

* * *

The cold air inside the mausoleum encircled Helena and her breathing misted in the air.

"Let me out!" Helena screamed and banged on the thick metal door.

Tears ran down her face as she hugged herself and crawled into a tight corner. She played mental checkers to occupy her thoughts. Sweat beaded on her forehead. The stench of hot urine traveled up her nose. It was the warmest she'd felt in hours. Helena got up and moved to a different corner.

She tried rubbing her hands together but it didn't help. *How long has Mom been gone*? Helena turned the flashlight on and off until the battery died. The air in the mausoleum thinned. A stream of snot dangled at the rim of her upper lip. She gasped with breaths that were unable to deliver the oxygen she needed.

The new world they lived in changed everything for the people who survived. They had to pay for the one thing they felt entitled to, *oxygen,* and no one was exempt. Everyone was fitted with a chip that acted as a delivery system to maintain healthy oxygen levels and to enforce the law. A tax for oxygen seemed less absurd in those moments when one's life depended on it. You never know how much your life depends on something until it actually does. The funny thing is Helena didn't have an implant like everyone else. She didn't need one, but everyone needs oxygen to survive.

* * *

It's been 12 years since Helena's death. After all this time they'd found Sarah buried beneath a coffin. Weeks later, Helena and her mother were buried next to each other in the same cemetery where they lost their lives. Lilac looked around at the funeral procession. Light conversation dotted the room and everyone was dressed in bright colors.

They were glad that they finally knew what happened to Helena and her family, but no one bothered to shed a tear. *People don't cry like they use to anymore.* Lilac and Nardo took a short stroll to a broad sycamore tree that stood off in the distance. The wind floated through her hair tossing a few stands to fall over her right eye. Nardo moved it aside and gently tucked it behind her ear.

"There's something I need to do. Come with me." She held his hand and they walked back to Helena's grave. They were the last ones left in the cemetery. Nardo opened a blanket that Lilac brought along, laid it next to Helena's grave and they sat down.

Nardo shot a peculiar glance at her. "What exactly are we doing?"

"Don't worry; we won't be doing anything wrong! We'll perform a ritual from the old religion that gives the dead a safe journey to the afterlife."

Lilac opened her bag and gave Nardo a cloak. "Put it on." They pulled the cloaks over their heads and Lilac held his hand.

"What's the incense for?" Nardo asked.

"It will cleanse her soul. Repeat after me: 'Go with the wind, take flight, enter the breast of the welcoming dove, into heavens light.'" Lilac lit a stick of lavender incense, stuck it at the base of the tombstone, along with the finished worry doll of Helena's likeness that she'd worked on for years.

ELEVEN

Three months had passed since the Garner's funeral, when a police car pulled up in front of the Paine's residence. Ruby saw the car from the kitchen window and went to the front door. She stood in the open doorway as Detective Baez walked up the porch steps.

"Good Afternoon Mrs. Paine. Is your daughter here?"

"She's upstairs. Is something wrong?"

"No, I just have a few questions to ask her."

"Lilac, Detective Baez is here to see you."

Lilac jogged down the steps and stop midway. "What's going on?"

"I have some additional questions about the Garner family." Lilac continued down the steps.

Ruby closed the door. "You can talk in the living room." They all went into the living room and sat down.

Detective Baez looked at Lilac as she sat beside her mother on the opposite chair.

"There are still some unanswered questions." He huffed. "The Garner's had many valuable items that were untouched. Robbery wasn't the motive. There's more to this story. I can feel it in my bones." He scratched his head. "Did your friend fill you in on why her family was killed?"

Lilac shook her head. "No she didn't. She only showed me her own death. She didn't know what happened to her parents and I don't think she knew why they were killed, otherwise she would have told me."

Officer Baez looked at her and sighed. "You're probably right. I'll continue to look into this."

* * *

The community was so focused on the Garner case that they completely forgot about the bodies found on Glen Street until the unsettling news came on the evening news segment. Police arrested members of a group called The Cleaners that had been secretly expanding in their town. The Cleaners were keen on raising hell in the community and on school campuses throughout Charleston. They infected the population by recruiting those who were susceptible to their agenda. Anyone who posed a threat to their way of life was eliminated.

A group of normal teenagers ran the group in Charleston, Oregon but they were in other states too. They despised Genmorph's but not for the reasons you may think. The lifespan of a normal was half of a Genmorph. They could live for a century given the right circumstances.

The Cleaners figured out that Genmorph's gave off a distinct odor. Those people, who they suspected were a part of the Genmorph population, were kidnapped and taken to the Glen Street warehouse. The twelve victims were just the first that the Cleaners were actively looking for, and when they found them, they would strap them to chairs and take their blood. They siphoned their blood into the flexible plastic bag used in medical facilities and they drained them until they stopped breathing.

Dealers sold their blood to underground crews who sold it by the ounce. The buyers would inject themselves with the blood. It gave them a euphoric high and increased their strength temporarily. When used in large quantities it induced mania that sent the user into fits of rage and they attacked anyone in sight.

The police got a break in the case when one of the culprits became juiced up on their supply, ran down the street naked, and attacked an elderly woman who was walking her dog, biting off the flesh of her cheek. She remains in critical condition at Mercy Hospital. A student from Vanderlin High School, Richard Tomlin was one of the first victims of the Glen Street murders.

* * *

Life in the Paine household was starting to return to normal, but Lilac and Ruby's relationship suffered a big blow from her deception. Lilac spent most of her time in the sanctuary of her room. She'd climb outside her window and gaze at the moon. It was a constant beacon of light in the darkest moments.

A part of her missed Helena, but she was happy that the Garner family was together at last. A lone tear fell from her eye. Helena spent over a decade looking for her mother, and Ruby was there in the next room and they barely spoke. Tears gushed from her eyes. She buried her head in the folds of her arms and rocked her body. Lilac crawled inside her window and ran to her mother's room. She burst through the door and hugged her mother.

"I love you Mom."

"I love you, too." Ruby let her own tears flow as she held her daughter close.

* * *

A year had passed since the Garner's were laid to rest. Ruby purchased their home for next to nothing after paying off the back taxes. The renovations were coming along better than she expected. It felt good to follow through with her husband Kent desires. It took time but the house came to life again and the community eyesore was no more.

For the most part, they had forgotten about the upheaval that happened in their lives the year before until a two-hour investigative televised special came on Channel 13 that featured Detective Baez and others connected to the case.

A fellow scientist, Dr. Robert Snow, had clashed with Geoffrey a few times, but they had put their differences aside for the greater good. Their views on the role science should play in the survival of the human race differed. Geoffrey believed in a self-sufficient society and Dr. Snow thought everything that happened to our world created a system that kept everyone in line. Unlike Geoffrey, Dr. Snow had a vested interest in keeping things as they were. His family owned the majority of shares in Remtec, the company responsible for providing their oxygen delivery and the collection of taxes.

Based on eyewitness accounts, Dr. Snow went inside Geoffrey's office for a case file that they were working on. Dr. Snow noticed a file with the title Omega Species. He opened it and found that it was about an animal species that Geoffrey had researched years earlier. He glanced through the file and the hairs on the back of his neck stood up. A photo of a strange creature, the size of a medium sized dog with gray skin that was hairless and had a large beak. Dr. Snow pulled a newspaper printed off the internet from behind the photo, 'Strange Creature Washes Up On A Netherlands Shore'. He tucked the file in the back of his pants and adjusted his clothing. Dr. Snow walked out with the other file in his hand and pretended as if everything was fine.

Later, in the comfort of his home, he looked through the file. He couldn't understand why Geoffrey would keep such an important find from him. It dawned on him as he looked at the dates in the file. Dr. Snow smirked; it coincided with a day he'd come to know over the years after hearing Geoffrey lament about the occasion.

The next day Geoffrey got a call from the lab; a fire had broken out and the building sustained smoke and water damage. Two days later, Sarah's doctor, Dr. Samuel was found dead in his home, bound to a chair. His business was vandalized and the bandits destroyed thousands of eggs from his clients.

Dr. Snow shared what he learned with his father, Godfrey Snow, the owner of Remtec. Godfrey wasn't about to let a child hinder his billion-dollar business. He hired someone to break into the lab and interrogate Dr. Samuel. He had a heart attack while they were torturing him.

Godfrey Snow had done more than that. He hired the three men and sent them to the Garner's home. Afterwards, they met with him at a secluded location in the hills on the outskirts of Charleston. They informed him that Sarah and Geoffrey were dead, but Helena got away. Mr. Snow wasn't pleased. He had the three men shot by his driver as they walked back to their vehicle. Later that day, police got a call of a fire on a road leading to private land.

Fire crews arrived on the scene and found a car on fire with three occupants. At the time, no one put the pieces together since the Garner's were never reported missing. Hair was found on Geoffrey Garner's clothing, and it was sent out to be tested and the DNA results were run for a match. It came up as a match for one of the men found in the burned-out car.

Dr. Snow was arrested. He had long moved on from his job working in the research lab and was now the vice president of Remtec. His father, Godfrey, was in a hospice dying from lung cancer. The police visited him at the center and questioned him. He died three days later. Dr. Snow's bail was set for a million dollars. The sum was paid and he was released from jail. Dr. Snow hasn't been seen since.

The Garner's deaths were more complicated than Officer Baez imagined. Helena's dad went against the grain. He'd broken the laws of science, but his reasons were far from selfish. Geoffrey and Sarah had been trying to conceive naturally for years, but they were unsuccessful. Sarah underwent In Vitro Fertilization, but unbeknownst to her, Geoffrey and Dr. Samuel had known each other for years. Geoffrey agreed to do something that had only been sanctioned by a committee prior.

He had come across a new species of animal that developed after the world changed. Through examination, he found out that the animal was both warm- and cold-blooded. It was unheard of and it had to be an error, but when he redid his testing the results were the same.

His unborn child was a new beginning for their family, but could also be a new beginning for their world. Geoffrey had the In Vitro Specialist inject the new animal DNA into his wife's eggs and had her artificially inseminated. They tried numerous times before the pregnancy was viable. Helena was an important piece in making the world whole again. They wouldn't have to pay for oxygen and the government would have less of a hold on their lives.

Little evidence remains, but Dr. Geoffrey Garner was also in the process of creating a vaccine that would eliminate their need for an oxygen delivery system to supplement the toxic air in the atmosphere. Instead, his ideas died with him. All of his files were destroyed in the fire. Also, before Sarah's deaths she had uncovered information about a group that branched out in their town called The Cleaners who were responsible for the murders of the 12 victims found at the Glen Street location.

Lilac sat on the sleigh couch for the entire two hours, listening to what they had to say. She wasn't much of a science geek, but she understood that anything that made them less dependent was a good thing. Helena was innocent; as far as she knew, she was normal and was no more important than anyone else was, but she was important to their survival. It's hard to imagine that one person can change the world and make it a better place, but there will always be someone that will do everything it takes to stop it from happening.

This world is different from the one you know, but like yours, no one knows what tomorrow holds. As Helena once said, 'If you're not willing to fight for what's right, you'll lose your rights. You'll miss out on all that you deserve.' Helena was robbed of her young life, but once we have entered this world and have passed on, we are never truly gone; we're simply transparent.

ABOUT THE AUTHOR

At the age of fifteen, S.J. Dennery began writing and before her sixteenth birthday she had accomplished her goal of being an author. Upon graduating high school she plans to pursue a career in the culinary arts.